The Double Task

Gray Jacobik

The Double Task

University of Massachusetts
Press ❧ Amherst

Copyright 1998 by

Gray Jacobik

All rights reserved

Printed in the United States of America

LC 97–32622

ISBN 1–55849–142–2

Designed by Edith Kearney

Set in Berthold Bodoni

Printed and bound by Braun-Brumfield, Inc.

Library of Congress Cataloging-in-Publication Data

Jacobik, Gray.

    The double task / Gray Jacobik.

      p. cm.

    ISBN 1–55849–142–2 (alk. paper)

    I. Title.

  PS3560.A249D6 1998

  811'.54–dc21   97–32622

                              CIP

British Library Cataloguing in Publication data are available.

for Bruce

ACKNOWLEDGMENTS

Grateful acknowledgment is made to the following magazines in which some of these poems first appeared, a few in different form. *Georgia Review*, "Skirts"; *North American Review*, "The Bed of Music"; *Ploughshares*, "Dust Storm" and "First Marriage"; *Southern Humanities Review*, "The Past"; *Alaska Quarterly Review*, "Funereal," "November," and "Figuration"; *American Literary Review*, "The Wooden Egg"; *Connecticut Review*, "The Composer," "The Last of Our Embraces Transformed from the First" and "Sylvia Plimack Mangold Paints"; *Prairie Schooner*, "Sappho's Voice"; *Sycamore Review*, "Brain Teasers"; *Southern Poetry Review*, "Sandwoman"; *Ontario Review*, "Turkeys in August"; *Alkali Flats*, "The Breakfast Room," and "The Circle Theatre"; *Louisiana Literature*, "The Movie Fan"; *Connecticut English Journal*, "Vines and Cathedral Lines"; *Nebraska Review*, "Flamingos"; *Pivot*, "Sappho Views Her X-Rays."

"Figuration" received a commendation from the National Poetry Competition, 1995; "The Reunion" received a commendation in the same competition in 1996.

"A Prelapsarian Mood Piece" received first prize and was published in the *1996 Emily Dickinson Award Anthology*, published by Universities West Press, 1997.

"The Breakfast Room" received The Yeats Prize awarded by the Yeats Society of New York, 1997.

"Dust Storm" was reprinted in *Best American Poetry, 1997* (New York: Scribners Paperback, 1997) and in *Anthology of Magazine*

Verse & Yearbook of American Poetry (Palm Springs, Calif.: Monitor Book Co., 1997).

"The Quilt Show" appeared in *Words & Quilts: A Selection of Quilt Poems* (Lincolnwood, Ill.: The Quilt Digest Press, 1996).

"Skirts," "Sappho's Voice," and "Sandwoman" were reprinted in *The Writing Path 2* (Iowa City: University of Iowa Press, 1996); "The Chinese Chestnut Breeze" appeared there for the first time.

The author wishes to thank The National Endowment for the Arts and the Connecticut Commission on the Arts for fellowships which supported the writing of many of these poems.

CONTENTS

One

Two

One

SKIRTS

Women spin and dance in skirts, sleep and wake
in them sometimes, ascend and descend stairs.
Some have walked into the sea in skirts,
which is like tossing a skirt over a man's head,
or pressing his face against the tent of one.
Some woman, maybe wearing a velvet skirt,
embraces another woman—so one skirt brushes
against another. Women wash and wring and hang
skirts up to dry, spray them, iron them, hem them,
slip them over slips, over tights. Once, I confess,
I owned six black ones: rayon, wool, gabardine,
linen, cotton, silk. The wind can blow the bulk
of a skirt between a woman's legs, or wrap her in
a twist, billow underneath so skirls of wind touch
faintly, delightfully. Some women hear skirts
murmuring or sighing, conversing with the flesh
they cover. But most skirts drape in silence, the silence
of slow snow falling, or the hushed liquid glide
of a woman's body through a sunlit pool, the sweet
descent to sleep, or passion, or passion's nemesis,
ennui. A woman's spirit lengthens or widens in a skirt,
magnified by cloth and cut and her stride through
the quickened space. If instead a woman wears
a tight skirt, she feels containment and its
amplification—reduction's power to suggest.

Right now my favorite is a crimpy cinnabar silk
I twist into wrinkles to dry. I wear it walking in
the evenings. I vanish as its folds enfold the sky.

SANDWOMAN

The woman lay firm in the damp berm of the beach—
she flowed into it and was contiguous with it,
was, in fact, formed of it. The sky chinked through
its hours, its gradations of sky-hues, the azures,
ceruleans, deeper blues, and the golds and roses
of evening. Sky was all she could see, all she
opened her legs to, all her breasts and belly strove
to touch. The sum of her changes were color
and cloud—until the lips of the sea reached her—
those lascivious lips bruised by the moon.
Seafoam threw its lace shawl over her shoulders
and fans of lace shrouded her face. Slowly, slowly,
in licks, and then sometimes in spills, the sea
overcame her, her wavy hair running down the beach,
right breast and then left breast crumbling like turrets.
Waves gathered back the seaweed of her pubis,
then licked at her sex until she dissolved the way,
so tasted, all women dissolve. She had given her
heart to the blinding smack of noonday light
and to the soft coruscations of the lamb-back clouds
that traversed her body through the late afternoon,
until she was only a shadow by night. The one who
shaped her with hands knew that love falls through
the body like sand, and the whole of the erotic sculpts
our limbs and faces, teases wide the splay of our legs.

SOUNDS DEEPER THAN HUMAN SILENCE

In the midst of looking up the word *ossuary* Paula said,
    give me a hug. I did, and later, standing on the porch,
        not smoking, she asked, did you ever notice how people

die around their birthday? It's an urn or vault for bones,
    which made me think of the poem about osso buco,
        about a restaurant with that name on the Lower East Side,

about Ben Webster's version of *In the Wee Small Hours*
    of the Morning, the way his reed quivers at the end.
        There's too much of life to take in, to do something with—

the rush of it over mind and body, the letting go.
    Paula said, so much for a Seven Sisters' education,
        then laughed—neither she nor Susan knew the word.

There again, the too-much to capture and the wish life
    might be containable the way human bones are,
        stripped of flesh, stripped of one-moment-on-the-heels-

of-another until one runs out of time. Ben Webster must have been
    a sad man who sometimes caught joy, sometimes got lifted
    on a cushion of soft air. Three days ago a stream

of blackbirds flew across my window perfectly horizontally
    so that they seemed to be lines with little blips on them
        like those on oscillographs in ICUs that show the failing

pulse. Once I did a pen and ink study of a shrunken head,
    a Maori tribesmen, his face tattooed to a paisley,
      and yesterday I saw a photo of a grimacing man

with the same designs on his face. I would like to walk down
    Madison Avenue some October day, *Early Autumn* playing
      in the Walkman, gazing from the flags to the buildings,

to the cafés and extravagant window displays, cabs strobing by
    like yellow bullets, most of it doubled in plateglass.
      I'd listen to the soft tenor blows expand out then

come back short through the long afternoon's gold light.
    Stephen Dedalus hears and registers nearly every sound
      in those portions of his life Joyce gives us, his world more

sound than sight, the *pick, pack, pock, puck* of the cricket bats.
    There's a certain striding I get into sometimes walking
      down a country lane or a city street, not exactly a swagger,

but as if forces were coming up from the ground or the pavement
    into my feet and thighs, hips and shoulders, power moving up
      and through the body of the woman walking. I'm as much

a statement then as I'm ever going to be. In the seventies
    I would sing *I Am Woman* booking down K Street
      in a plaid flannel shirt, jeans, workers' boots,

in the city from the commune, but this morning I sang
    O What a Beautiful Morning because it was.
        High white clouds but blue breaking through,

the shimmer-green of a late cool spring.
    The strength and fragility of music cradled then dandled.
        In the one picture I have of Webster, he's wearing

a hepcat's zoot suit, baggy pants ballooning down to spats.
    His tie is abundant and lavish in its printed swirls. He's not
        smiling, he's looking down at his golden sax.

THE BUCK IN THE SNOW

Wings flap to eat, twenty crows to eat the entrails
of the buck that must have struck a car, perhaps
your red Honda wrecked last fall, hitting the deer that
surprised the road, that surprised you heading home.

Now it rots in our woods where this morning the dogs
scattered a cabal of crows that in one swift-flapping
ascension rose. Twenty black capes in diverse directions,
crows with entrails in their beaks like little bloody

banners: *here is the death that struck the car.* Death nearby,
near us, the buck snow-capped in its pied coat,
a callus on its ear, six-points. So the woods blurred
with stench or they started to smoke, tricolored entrails

sprayed from the anus on the snow, crow-picked over,
crow-splayed, a calligraphic dance of clawed feet,
hieroglyphs untranslatable, but who knows? The buck
looked in our bedroom window on its way to the

three white pines past the beech, looked at us asleep,
hushed in weariness, blankets undulant with dreams.
Then the dogs barked. There with us now and
forever, the buck under the quilt, under the snow.

No place to go without the buck—it struck your car,
looked through our window, came into our bed
to die there. Death has moved in and over us,
spread its dark cape, says it will caw in our bones.

SAPPHO'S VOICE

I love the traffic of percussives in her voice,
her susurrations, her fricatives, the wave slaps
and ululations that run counterpoint, polyphonous

syllables that lift to words that run to sentences
so dazzling in intonation, one thinks of angels
with silver tablets on silver laps composing

under olive trees in the Mediterranean of
the soul's true home. Well, she is a perfect
creature, a *creatura*, formed for poetry's sake,

so one ought to expect her voice to spill
across her lips as fluidly as water slips across
a lip of fountain stone or drips from the tips

of olive leaves after summer storms. I would
lick each drop, each word as it slips, filling
my spirit with the sound of her good sense.

Can grace turn on a voice, the way a body turns,
grace and the body in a kind of auditory spin,
or spinning flight that makes soundwaves its sky?

Her voice leaps with light turned back upon itself,
light turning to sound then back to light—
now desire, now the mind's surrender to desire.

SAPPHO VIEWS HER X-RAYS

Nothing here Anaktoria could cherish, not
even this pelvic cradle is clearly mine, nothing
to prize—dense bone, shadows, and some
silver fillings.

Dissolved the eyes she called obsidian magnets,
and my clitoris, her jewel, now a shadow
folded in a shadow, like the lining of
a silken glove—

my belly is a bowl of dark-gray light. Here,
the grid on which desire plots its dreams,
sketches elaborate schemes, strategizes,
compels its compromises.

No violets or lacy chervil can garland this sere
frame. And somewhere, perhaps in marrow, words
drift by like crying revenants among the
crevices and hollows.

Surely poems are nascent in these branches, moon
poems silvered and writhing through this mystical
nightwood. I hear them wail like animals who
give birth in trees.

THE PAST

Always a carnival at midnight and the lights
        of rides turning off one-by-one. Lingerers
moving slowly toward parked cars, then night
        gives its dust back to the dry fields.
They drove out and parked in the cornfields.
        In his back seat, they kissed and pressed
their bodies into one another. The wind, warm
        and clotted with summer, razzed
through cornsilk. When he lifted himself over her,
        when he entered her, stars came down
through his hair. Something swerved off-course,
        spiraling-up like stray particles or whizzing by
like a fly—a departing world, she will come to believe,
        that farm boy's world. Years later, walking under
evening clouds, silver-rimmed like those Turner
        or Constable painted, clouds above country lanes
that curved into shadows, she lay down and slept
        for an hour. A brook with a name like Nightingale
or Abington soothed her with its water-trapped
        sweet-talk. Then she woke from her nap
and brushed her clothes as if nothing had happened,
        but another world had swerved off and she
was no longer a part of it. Every hundred journey-miles
        the past is halved by Ockham's Razor, now-grainy
images sheered once more, sliced thin as mica or forced
        into shadows like thieves—so we keep going,

exchanging our present world for a new one—
    a decision, an insight, but sometimes unwittingly,
as if the cosmos flipped over and we became someone
    new. Wholly elsewhere, we resume our lives—
the trade invisible and simple, indivisible, absolute.

DARKNESS

The first half-minute when the retina retains traces
of light—glowing spheres or floaters under eyelids:
false light, true light. Thunder in my hands.

Once a stranger rubbed against me in a crowded
elevator and ejaculated on my skirt. I thought he wet
himself and me because he was sick. Girlie! Girlie!

—another man cavorting in a silly clunky way,
like Pinocchio waving his penis. So darkness crests,
becomes part of the complaining limbs of trees.

Striated darkness. Opaque darkness. Darkness with
complex gradations. Bat-black, crushed velvet gloom,
bibulous privacy. Night can lick you with its strong

metallic tongue, make a sop of you, leave you
blueberry patinaed, swat you earthward, your passion
a broken kite punched down by a swift gust.

We settle into darkness, welcoming night, or is this
the one we would stave off forever? Open the door.
Drift into shadow. Darkness. Linger on the bridge

over the dim water, jump in or row out,
take a swim. In the Susquehanna one June night,
the phosphorescence never before so up-river,

our bodies like bales of light sliding through water,
hair aglow, hands fountaining light. Goddess talc
caught in the moon's wake, the waves' cups,

caught by the lamp at the end of the dock.
When mowers cut the brush along the road, they
exposed a quail's nest. Safe in the vegetation

with her brood, now panic in her red-rimmed eyes.
I broke cattails and willows in the brake, carried her
as much as I could. Darkness grievous in my arms.

A sinister darkness, intrusive, impossible to shake.
Down, down, down, rappelling into night—
hand-over-hand across impossible ropes. I would

have laughed but knew to turn and run. Now,
under the porch light snow shapes the black
space between each flake, *claire-obscure*, and no

volition or surrender or intention. The lightning
above the storm, the world turning shock pink,
bright blue—a final dark blooming above clouds.

FUNEREAL

Twice today I spied huge crows ripping
a small creature apart, flapping off
over the pines like aerial hearses. I think
of the Shelleys in Venice, a gondolier
poling them through the canals, the dead
child in Mary's arms. Nothing deep enough
to change us comes easily, sometimes first it
petrifies us. Late February light is a blessing—
maybe grace acknowledges itself this way.
Between patches of woods, ice fields, glazed
and crusted, tatters of mist wisping over the roads.
Chipmunks, moles, mice must be venturing
from stonewall crevices, foraging across the crust,
daring whatever kills them, the cat perhaps.
How did the façades of the palazzos strike
those two that afternoon, a stark late winter
light, gliding in that black funereal gondola?

FLAMINGOS

Delicate as the inside color of a conch,
    they are offered to us mirrored by the lake.
        We can almost extend our hands and smear
            the flaming muted light. There, at lake's edge,

they sieve their ambrosial lunch,
    cranking up elbowed knees, lifting
        awkward S-curved necks, tipping drowsy
            oval bellies. They are about to take off

between those ancient arboreous ladies,
    cypresses draped in Spanish moss.
        They are almost not there, or the lake's not,
            or we're not. Suppose they mistake lawn

for lake, lily-stalked, lost in their blossoming
    motion? Suppose they rose awkward as angels,
        taking their cotton souls away,
            veering into the absence of flamingos?

TURKEYS IN AUGUST

At the bramble-end of the car lot, five wild turkeys,
a cock and four hens, ragged looking, solemn.
Rusting car parts season the soil. Morning glories
enscroll the chainlink, each blossom a small moon
the bees sail to. A strip of bluebonnets and asters,
goldenrod coming into bloom. Decay everywhere
and beauty too—the unravelings and knittings
of the world. Once the Nipmucks lived on this land
stewarded now by Hyundai and Toyota, and in between,
eight generations of emigrants: millers, farmers, millworkers.
A row of Cressidas, a model replaced by Avalons, names
that suggest medieval romance and Arthurian paradise:
Cars are dreams that pass in succession. Amid islands
of dumped tires, the turkeys roost. A pool of oily water
rainbows when wind quivers the light. A few yellow locust
leaves break, twirl down slowly, yellow falling through blue,
falling past green. Nothing redemptive in this scene:
We want the paradise we can buy, not the one given,
and no one's taken to task for sinning against land.

BRAIN TEASERS

The long glass table after dinner,
my husband and his grown sons
and their wives solve puzzles:
three theologians debate the nature

of an abyss—one slips, another coughs,
the third sighs, who is the infidel?
Or, if A is a liar and B always tells
the truth, is C the experienced archer?

I listen and serve strawberries, serve cream,
coffee. Evening's light glows lemon
and rose. Their competing voices
reason and propound—waves smashing,

streams blurting, brooks, silence,
silence broken. Is the pea
under the third shell a wiser choice
than the goat inside the woodshed?

Will the second émigré prosper or only
his descendants? Behind them on the
sideboard, the daylilies slowly seal
their orange-red cups. Daylight paces

away from the window, passes along
the garden, enters the tenebrous wood.
Six sailors jump ship, five drown,
which one held a lock of his sweetheart's

hair? Is it further to the poppy field
or to the old man's tomb? Enigmas
resolved into the soft night's
steep hours. The stars remain quiet.

I dream of a dazzling maze carved in snow.
Through it—millions of perfect bodies
turn and twist and drift—uncanny dancers
following the tinkling bell of a scruffy goat.

THE DISCOVERY

The woman who hovers in the upper left with a veil
or mantle over her head may be the Phoenician
moon goddess Astarte. The bodies writhing low

and center echo earlier forms, fallen angels in
Blake's first and seventh illustrations of *Paradise Lost*.
Entangled in seaweed, a raging mermaid—

beside her, two dragonfly nymphs, hair entwined
into crossing comet tails. Humans in diaphanous
robes drift mid-region through crepuscular light.

Surely here's the psyche of the engraver-poet
whose spiritual crises were so ample we've yet
to come to terms with all he felt: torments

and ecstasies, his glimpses of an imperiled Eden,
the hope of fruitful union he suggests with flocks
of sheep grazing on hills, and all that bucolic brouhaha

that seems fanciful to us, if not, at times, deranged.
Had Blake's generation had Prozac or the tricyclics,
he might not have given us what we now revere,

nor have flourished the fractious mixtures of techniques
and tastes scholars are pleased to call Romanticism.
We did not know then how to inhibit seratonin re-uptake,

although we knew Satan and the universal cycles
of time leading to apocalypse. Cutting in from left
and right, flowers with whimsical wandering stems

and wild petals flayed open like parrot tulips left
a week in a vase, curvilinear, proclaiming one
of Blake's most sacred beliefs: line is, at all times,

superior to color, although he, or Catherine, experts
think, would have simply and delicately, hand-tinted
these carnelian. Next week an artist in relief-etched

printing is going to have a go at this, so the world
as prison for the human spirit that requires release,
will release his vision, engraved in reverse in copperplate

two hundred years ago, and with an extravagance of luck,
stumbled upon in a chimney sealed since the 1830s, London
ardent for condos: This glory Blake made bastion against his fate.

LOST TRAINS

One seldom hears a train these days, hallooing
out to the night or to town or village, declaring
its advent and warning wandering creatures
to flee or pay the consequences. Few *Night Owls*
on Amtrak, few true plug runs either, no *Bullet,*
no *Cannonball,* no *Streamlined Flyer.* Passenger
trains haul only coach cars these days, pulled by
the stalwart engine. No parlor cars, hopper cars,
no more cabooses. And what of the tender,
that boxy tank for coal and water coupled behind
the engine? Its name couldn't save it from oblivion.
No baggage cars anymore, only overhead racks,
and the dining car is a snackbar that sells beer
and soft drinks, pretzels and other munchies.
And in America, at least, it's hard to come by
a sleeper—a Pullman divided into roomettes.
How sleek those pressed sheets felt—the privacy
curtain drawn—a lullaby of rattling windows
and the comforting *click-pocka click-pocka* that
vibrated your berth. No more jiggling moon
angling through clouds, sliced by the poles
you count falling asleep, wheat fields or mountains
or rivers, perhaps St. Louis or Chattanooga sliding
alongside your body blanketed close to the glass.

THE DOUBLE TASK

Raining as it rained yesterday, as it rained last night—
and we want the song to go on forever, loop round

and come back, song without end, a baritone's song
to pester the heart's sacred wishes, a mournful song

but sweet in its sublime reaches. A piercing recollection.
I told her as I had the day before, the best songs pierce,

poignant thrusts again and again to the core, the soul's
true haven. Baritones' voices are always poignant,

baritones' and mezzo-sopranos'—the mid-ranges.
You might think highs and lows most piercing, but not so.

The middle ground, the middle way, the aural terrain
you can get lost in. Long notes that hold sway over longings

and desires. I had two songbirds once, one the double
of the other, both vivid green with yellow underwings.

Those birds sang and sang—high notes, low notes, twitterings
and chirps. A cage in front of a mirror that reflected a mirror

reflecting morning light, so they sang mornings as if mornings
were what song was for. Their cage shook with warblings and

bird chortles, low notes in rapid succession, high notes that,
if louder, might have shattered that silvered glass. No middle

notes from those birds, for that we have baritones. Baritones
with chests that barrel forth, and mezzo-sopranos with formidable

bosoms, singers who strut as if they're bracing the sea's most
tempestuous waves. Glorious singers in their stage dress—

shimmering gowns, tuxedos that make the baritones look
like great auks. The world's aflood with singers, all repeating

lyrics. Myself, I like opera. So like walking into an orchard
in bloom. So like deep-sea diving through coral caves. The Italian.

The German. A total immersion in the artifice of glory.
Conventions laughable if you think about them, but of course

you don't, you dive in, you swim, you ride the sky waves of blossoms
or the sea waves of seas and imagine you're resting your head

on that woman's glorious bosom or warming in the radiant heat
of that baritone's chest. Much of opera is about repetition

and recurrence—refrains tell us the parts we should long
remember. Words come back, sounds come back, the rain comes

again as it did yesterday, the rain of today was here last year,
new canaries hatch from canary eggs and they are green,

they are yellow, some blue born of blue ones. The same operas
are re-staged and we play the tapes again, we play the CDs,

we play the video of Puccini's *Turandot*, not once, never only once.
Apple blossoms drift like last year's blossoms drifted and this

going on for decades, somewhere since the beginning. The rain
evaporates and returns to the seas, then ascends and comes back

to us. Recurrence, repetition, and so you believe in the Eternal
Return and reincarnation and all that Vico said about history and

cycles and Yeats of great wheels and gyres and what astronomers
believe about worlds-onto-worlds and flip-over universes extending

through multiple infinities and the relation of time to space and
space to time and of forms emerging from and disappearing into

the formlessness of voids, the vortices of black holes where all the
music ever sung swirls around in astral aviaries splashed with stars.

*T*wo

A PRELAPSARIAN MOOD PIECE

A city stands as the mind's most distinct heritage,
the way Erik Satie, accused once of formlessness,
sat down and wrote *Composition In The Form of a Pear*.
Two striking women holding hands, walking, laughing,

lost in themselves, the way a city can undo one's wise
intentions, streets ambling past shops and parks
and flower stalls. The famous Saint-Gaudens statue
in Rock Creek Cemetery, called *Grief*, is Mrs. Henry Adams,

Clover, who poisoned herself with potassium cyanide
she used in developing photographs. She is downcast,
broken as if nothing of happiness remained in the world.
Once I made love in the house she poisoned herself in,

sitting in an overstuffed chair, horsehair upholstery.
The Triangle Club now, corner of 16th and something.
I was a guest of a visiting dignitary. We dignified the bed.
We dignified the chair. When one looks into the face

of *Grief* one's spirit flies out as if a thousand grackles
hurled themselves from one's chest and flew up amid
raucous untamed flappings. Not this music I weave
through my hair, music in the shape of a pear. My mother

married in a peagreen dress with a little peagreen pillbox
hat, veil rhinestone-studded. I have roamed this city
of rainy mornings, then placed pears on the sideboard,
listened to Satie hour after hour. Satie and rain,

mornings and pears. Up on the roof, Amy sang
Up On The Roof to me when she was breaking up with
Jonathan. The city rose before us, the Lord's best
marvel, pied in its mottled clouds and rain-struck

puddles of light. It was too much like a Rauschenberg
to be real. She honeymooned in Richmond, sealing
hope, forgetting war and all prior loneliness and she
conceived me, or conceived of me, if not then, soon.

Stoned out of my mind I would wander down to Dupont
Circle and listen to the Black men singing old Platters'
and Drifters' tunes. Such harmonies escalate elations.
The light that can sheer a cliff can sheer an office

building, sheered the Building of Lost Causes where
all the hippies worked, where I worked once, saving
the tides from coastal encroachments. Up in the elevator
to the top of doom, down later to the tobacconist.

THE CHINESE CHESTNUT BREEZE

for Sonja Weber

The fragrance weaves through the painter's studio,
surrounds the bright-white canvas on her easel.
Perhaps she's a nihilist, or an existentialist,

bound to project an unrivaled view. No lines.
No colors. No shapes except the chaste format:
an oblong so long it shows the full extension

of her history. Perhaps she has painted the light
we pass into when we meet pure extinction.
In she walks. Observes and waits. She turns on

Handel's Water Music. Black cat flexes then sleeps
on the windowsill, framed by the many-tasseled
green canopy awash in wind. Some say the smell

is pleasing-sweet—some are sickened by it, the tree
blooming in spiral clusters that flop open in jumbled
arrays. Too much. Too sexual. Provoked by Handel,

the painter's caged starling sings. At last, the dichotomies
have aligned themselves in sensuous display:
light and dark—sound and silence—sweetness, sickness.

SYLVIA PLIMACK MANGOLD PAINTS

Light falls through all its serious permutations—
    stippling the limbs of elms and cottonwoods,
    trickling evening down the eastern edges of bark.

In the beginning, linen stretched tight. In the
    beginning, paint. A frame-within-a-frame-
    within-a-frame so field undercuts ground,

tension shifts left or right depending on the fear
    that weighed on her the day the composition
    complained. Erasures cease to exist, but what else

call these shadow decisions left to mark the history
    of thought? She paints on the masking tape,
    faux-tape, making a joke of containment.

No art without a frame, Magritte said, only the long
    considered game of division. Sky-blue pinks flow
    to pale roses that flow to gold. Ashes become creams.

A hint of cloud heaves a sky—but that's next year's work.
    Three cypresses unstring the more expansive
    oaks. Aerial dimensions address aerial dimensions.

Evening commences when crimson strikes, and the line
    of mountains that broke across the eye of the
    woman, breaks: The image renounced for the sake

of vision. Beyond the distractions of dross, the sly
fulgurations of matter, she studies the scene and
compounds it. All views past survey, past speech.

THE QUILT SHOW

Among these lozenges, rhomboids, and octagons
of cotton, love is bound by *Double-Wedding Rings*,
the heavens brightened with Feathered Stars.

Like mazes or puzzles or Goldbach's conjectures,
intelligence burgeons, seeks in pleasing patterns
and colors, an underlying order, a true design.

Grandmothers' Fans cool wrinkled faces
while the young are tied in *Lover's Knots*.
Alone, in odd hours, through the long months,

a woman sews zigzag, sawtooth or parallel stitches,
or secures the cotton waddling in concentric
circles—life within a life, child within a womb.

On its frame, the quilt spreads, a globe wrapped
in *Double-Irish Chains*, or in gradual shades,
light steps down through squares of *Tumbling Blocks*.

Beside a *Log Cabin*, or a *Yankee Puzzle, Cottage Tulips*
bloom. A quilt on the bed says: the woman who made me,
encircles you, she wishes you a peaceful night. Dream
of *Cathedral Windows, Plaid Mountains, Broken Stars*.

FIGURATION

for Robert Sargent

Five crows trade treetops in the bare woods,
a carrion-eater's musical chairs, triangular
perch exchanges with excursions to and from

the fallen leaves. Light black bodies gliding
with ease, the hop-to winglift comes, sometimes,
accompanied with caws. Not harbingers or omens,

not portents or blessings, my wily self this morning
wants to see them as crows, so puts me in mind of
my friend, Bob, the poet, who eschews metaphor

as a side-stepping gesture, appropriating,
arrogant. But I love transformations of all kinds
and so we've argued round it for years. The thing

itself, and naming precisely, he'd say, the
consummate stroke: crows, five sleek black ones,
trading places in trees. Playing musical chairs

I counter, each chair upholstered in silver brocade,
a bit rococo, and to an ornithological Bach cantata
programmed into their craniums—or a pack

of crow-faced tarot cards guides their shuffled
places, randomly assorted by the divining skies.
Boundary-marking crows, now moving deeper

and finally out of sight, heralding the bare-branch
season, I want to say—cawing, he'd say, and not
for any human reason: crows cawing in trees.

LINES

When snow's on the ground I walk toward tangled
places—briars and vines, the second-growth thickets
of once-cleared fields. I locate bittersweet that climbs
high in half-dead trees, loops in spills, probes tendrils
along wires. I watch for the scribble of winterberry—
shapes one might sharpen a pencil for, doodle down
a page. I've lost myself by a wall tracing the conical caps
and ridges of each stone, the rude diagonals of a toppled
cord of wood. Grace tracing lines, as if one moves
closer to primal design, the Lord a draftsman first.
Ups, downs, lefts, rights, slow curving climbs and swift
rounded falls, dizzying spirals, the music and motion
of sight driven to define itself in the sparest of terms.
Line refreshes when we're overwhelmed by the boisterous
play of color and mass—the sketch that leads us back
to what the mural will become. Perhaps it's most
like reading, the way our eyes move the mind along a line
that turns and proceeds at a varying pace, the pleasures
of poetry over prose, a proclivity hard-wired in us that grants
shape to thought and feeling, or an earlier claim—the need
to follow a path. I'm happy walking in snow, taking in
the fluent borders of forms, the pattern vision traces.

THE BREAKFAST ROOM

She has looked at him in the way of fire, of roses,
in light that spills suspension onto morning's table,
room with the fricative name, room of luxury
come round as if they were stars from the forties,
he in satin robe, one hand on the folded paper
and unopened mail, she in silk kimono and beaded
slippers. Silver service on a silver tray and the
firewalk of deathlessness that comes between them.
Light buffs the mahogany amber, biscuits and honey
and cream, coffee and bacon, daisies in a willowware
pitcher, an open window, and beyond, the garden
perfectly tended, yesterday's blooms open and buds
to unfold today, each cupping small prisms, the fire
of light that comes in July, in June, and fire that is
intelligence, the self's story of life, fire as it gambols
along the strands of love that flow from one person's
eyes to another's, fire that rushes the skin's galvanized
surface when beloved touches beloved. He kisses her
forehead and one of them notices the year, the decade,
ephemerality become tangible, as if a century from now
they were looking at a painting rendered in the style
of the Pre-Raphaelites, *The Breakfast Room*, rich in its
chinoiserie, a silver service, a kimono, terrace beyond
French doors, the last instant before Whistler when
every brushstroke was still a fact—the swift collapse
when the beloved recalls winter, or fear, the cankerous
sore that will corrode the spirit most becalmed into flesh.

She studies films about cooks, but the aromas
never attend the illusion, films clotted with

chopping and clanging pots and the final squawks
of squab or guinea-hen as the chef 's apprentice

wrings its neck, a few yaps from bamboo-caged
dogs—films of deceiving waifs, clever gypsies,

lovers rived from one another by those who
covet love, or trains crammed full of Hindus

Muslims blow up, or Muslims Hindus blow up—
sixteen hundred years of hatred reduced to

splattered dye. She relishes lavishly costumed
dramas and close-up conversations in interior spaces,

subtle twitching of eyelid or lip—and the desire
that roves her body as she leaves the theatre,

walks through mist, drives home in night's dark
capsule. Later, kissing him, the extravagance

of scent. Wertmuller and Polanski taught her
never confess infidelity over surges of romantic

music. Was it lonely afternoons in Rome reading
French subtitles that gave her to worship a pace

slower-than-life—foregrounds of meticulous detail?
He thinks these tedious films of talk and texture—

but she feels the mercurial drift of manners lost,
a-fast-slide-to-dream. Even her past, now, seems

like outtakes someone's clipped and swept to
the incinerator, not as true as Fellini's peacock

fanned in the snowy plaza, his dandelion puffs
drifting past a wedding party, a flamenco dancer's

skirt smoldering, the peasants too frenzied to
notice. Once, watching *All That Heaven Allows*,

the film caught fire, a brown crinkle melting
to white savagely, as if the world she saw ending

in a flash had been filmed, too, and no place left to
return to, a cold scream of light all the ever to ever be.

Summer has ascended into heaven trailing its divine
and perfect days, a season becalmed at the blue hand
of the Virgin—Our Lady of the Compassionate Gaze.
Old man gone now a quarter century, and gone those
end-of-summer days in that old Italian millworker's

creation and blessing, tended evenings, row-upon-row.
Angels above the ripening fruit, or spirits gathering in
a whited flock near the distant end. World without end,
burgeoning, swift with power, a faith quick as bees, and
saints with contorted faces still live and die on this soil.

Screams any season cut through a god's collapse.
Hear the pipes and hollow mouths, each a cry for his
unending resurrection, and in the evenings a vineyard
to tend, chimes, and the goldenrod sway of the lighted
air. Fluted lines carry vision upward—every line

of the cathedral ascends, rays of radiant light, tendril
and vine, carved tips of angels' wings, the channeled
columns, volutes, capitals, higher and higher
to the gold-domed roof. A siphoning of spring
water, almost audible—a hillside filled with light,

and light lining gnarled knobby vines, leaves softly fuzzed,
tendrils spiraling above the bright clusters. Asters
and heal-all strewn mid-row. White joy and laughter
at the purple quick. Infinity beyond—and beyond, a field
of goldenrod, wind-waves soughing, the liquid lessons

motion speaks. October leaves tinish-gold and thin,
grapes harvested by those gnarled Italian hands,
his knife snipping each bunch so deftly you would think
the sky was falling. November sunset viewed from that cold-
wrapped vine-hovelled hill, the deep-pink and orange

domains slashed by long grey clouds. The hollow pipes
of the organ, each with a screaming mouth, a Munch mouth,
and saints pierced, stoned, burning, calling to the dour
mournful sufferer whose body folds in the most eloquent
of collapses, loosened from his cross, carted to his tomb.

FIRST MARRIAGE

Drought summer I broke my foot and hobbled on crutches.
Stood staring, crutches against the counter, refrigerator door
open, blank light spilling. Your mother, all hours, weeping
upstairs, her widow's heart splitting her chest apart.
Home after nine, or later, vacant as a ghost, you would swallow
me with a hot mouth, grime visible on your neck, your hands.
A tire dropped like a scream from the beech, then the children's
sandbox with its litter of plastic toys, the rusted jungle gym.
A clothesline that spun and squeaked in storms. Two neighbor
farms against the sky to the north, but everything else blank.
Crickets, and louder, cicadas, and still louder, frogs.
Sometimes cows lowing or the long low wail of the freight
trains passing through Carmargo. Was it the foolishness
or the emptiness that mattered? Remember the barn swallows
chirping before dawn and how happiness entered us then
as rapidly as spring took the prairie? Milk soured so quickly
and I would scrub that kitchen till it glistened and a silence
opened in the long afternoons. Some days I longed to bite
into the light and vanish. Light brushing windows, stepping
across the paneled walls. The old torn couch on the porch,
you over me and forcing me and with cars passing a half-mile
off—your mother upstairs—the thrumming of sixteen-wheelers.
You sold feed. You traveled. The sky passing new clouds
east and they would thin out and dissolve, or gather illuminated
in the evenings, or in the afternoons, heavy and dark with rain.
After all the cats died and your mother went back to Florida,
a dizziness once, watching the dust a truck blew up and wind

carried off, the baby asleep in his playpen, dogs not barking.
Blue chicory behind the barn, Queen Anne's lace, goldenrod.
This happened. I lived there with you. We were young, stumbling
and half-asleep in our existence on this earth. There were children.

DUST STORM

A secret like a lodestar, a ball of pure lead, I thought
about tasting him long enough for a life to wither,
a new planet to come into view. I imagined the smell
of his genitals, so common, so indescribable.
Wyoming and summer. Thunderheads galloping
in a stark yellow light. Or puffball clouds white
as eggs streaming over eye-piercing cobalt skies.
Grasses and hyssop. Jewelweed and coneflower.
Through the long evenings we would lean against
fences telling our lives more precisely than they had
ever been told. Desire rang bell-deep in my pelvic bone.
Two foxes loping along a ridge, or two coyotes.
Moon licked clean the sleek backs of his geldings.
Wherever I slept, my body spiraled then glided.
Distant ancestors appeared in dreams and spread
embroidered robes and silken scarves before me,
opened lacquered boxes filled with blue dust.
The prairie winds caught that dust. Even the crickets'
scrapings grew muted. One can over-think a thing.
The road skirled dust into tiny funnels, the funnels
to waves, the waves to a sea. I never slept with him,
but grew remote as a watch. Windswept plains,
sagebrush, tumbleweeds, and later, contrails
that crosshatched a shock-pink sky. His cattle
began to look painfully dumb. All were castrated.
My blood had grown too thin in Wyoming's thin air.
A woman out of her element, adrift on a high plateau.

And the heavy green of these summer trees,
on this Earth with its seasons and weathers,
the great panorama around and above and below,

a long soft rain fell during the night. By nine,
tatters of mist were a scrim against returning fields.
Grasses and flowers sprung upright as the heaviness

of rain lifted away. Moles burrowed in the ground,
beetles shed their larval shells and clawed up toward
the heat. A light breeze, and all afternoon small

scalloped white clouds in a slow scamper eastward,
a clarity as if everything near were in a Dutch still life,
and everything far part of a luminist landscape.

Cows waded up to their fetlocks in the pond,
caught the cool current in their dewlaps. When they lifted
their heads water trickled from their mouths in small

flashing streams. Evening, and an ethereal cleanness.
The angled light scaled and tinged the rims and ridges
of clouds. From the horizon to the top of the dome,

gold, rose, and blue moved up through a thousand
progressively darker shades. Goldfinches, sparrows,
and swifts crossed and recrossed, then later, hidden,

chirped as nightfall unfolded and closed the day.

THE COMPOSER

In Fall River an old woman plays a piano—
notes fly up chaotically like birds with
torn wings. A cotton river of enormous

tropical flowers, her printed robe, falls
over the piano bench. Some notes rest on
the backs of chairs, some on the shoulders

of the silver-haired women who have come
to the dayroom to hear the composer play.
Their hands pinch and poke, trying to pick

the gaudy over-sized flowers that splatter
on their robes like dropped water balloons.
Each wants to carry a bouquet back to her room,

then gaze at the river that falls from view
and fades to nothing in the summer light.
Beyond the windows birds flutter in trees,

drop suddenly, heavily, to the silver grass,
or vanish in light that shines from the river.
A silver August morning and the hot flowers

long for the brusque kiss of frost. The black
blades of fans whir like bats before caves.
The composer's voice, ephemeral as snow

in August, is pitched high as glass trinkets
that shatter. Once, in the thirties, walking to
a Radio City audition, panic scratched her

thin bones. Smoke blew from the Camel sign
over Times Square, and she felt the tumble
and swirl of music before it vanishes in air.

The Camel man's mouth in its firm stiff *O*
promised her a new life if she'd stop singing.
Now her thin fingers skim the ivory keys,

her fragile voice, ghostly as premonition,
sings of her losses. Her audience picks
at cloth flowers and gums thin vanishing

lips that crave frost. One-by-one, tottering,
or shuffling in slippers, silver women carry
bouquets back to their rooms, then stand

washed out in life's silver river.

THE ELECTION

Crushed velvet chair, overstuffed, peagreen,
  from the Salvation Army store—my salvation
  to sit there through one long October afternoon

watching light play across the wall painted velvet,
  no, painted lavender—the floor painted grey
  with silver-grey deck paint—to sit silent enough,

patient, unstirring, to wait. A shotgun apartment
  in a courtyard eight blocks from the Capitol,
  Eighth and A Streets, the whole of the Western

world astir through the windows, city of secret
  collaborations. Light firing the air, fire on the
  Reflecting Pool repeating the seagulls swirling

above the Capitol, and moving, changing—across
  the wall, along the floor, velvet floor, silver
  wall. The day before, in Weston, Massachusetts,

a woman wearing her mother's old fur coat,
  drinking vodka, got into her garaged red Cougar,
  turned on the ignition, then invited the priest

of oblivion into her body. Not a great poet, this
  woman alive a day ago—self-absorbed, fantastical,
  too fearful—but she'd have to do—the nearest

closest predecessor and besides, an impelling force
　　dry as wind, a hacking cough, a deep raspy laugh,
　　brushed the woman in the crushed velvet chair

when the spirit of the poet, no longer male or female,
　　whirled at the speed of light out of this world.
　　Having for my soul's sake come to poetry, for poetry's sake

come to my soul, light moving over the lavender wall,
　　the city of brethren bought and sold, of brethren
　　broken and soiled, the sigh of the world that inflates

the bones, light gone mad, a woman driven mad by fear,
　　gone into the dark wake of her pain, into the eternal
　　sorrow that lulls and wakes, wakes and lulls—yes, said

the young woman when evening finally came, when wind
　　ceased and the stir of the city calmed—yes, yes, I will account
　　for the claims she made and abandoned: I will do it.

New people are born into the world who resemble
old people long in the world, and the genetic pool
is large enough now so a nose comes back, a gait,
a cleft chin even if some one person, or a family

of persons, fails to reproduce. Alix's face appears
in an eighteenth-century portrait. I saw your loved
body walking within another's soul—my mother's hair
exalting a stranger's head. Auburn curls in cascades

like falls. The way she would stand parochial-school
stiff in her navy nurse's cape, lips pursed for a kiss:
a woman contained in self's form. Nothing binding
endures. Countess Olenska was not a Pfeifferesque

blond, but flawed, imperfectly beautiful, yet beautifully
protective of the innocent, and her wit could undercut
grandiose pretensions. Do some see the naked breast
beneath a sweater or tunic, suggested by jacket, dress,

blouse, how it falls, is pressed, moves, a particular
petulance? I was days up the Albanian coast before
I remembered giving her my navigation charts for
the pea coat she slipped over me that chilly morning.

We lost ourselves in that fog. The famous "pink coat"
was named not after the color, which is scarlet, but
Mr. Pinque, the tailor who designed it for aristocrats
to wear while hunting foxes. We named our Shetland

Sheepdog Adam Olenska after Madame. . . . If I say
he looks British to me, I mean long cheeks and long nose,
sallow skin, high forehead, a pleasant rectitude of bearing,
colorless hair. I like to see blond women wearing red,

dark-haired women dressed in black. Yuki, on the
other hand, was unusual for an Asian because she
walked inside her clothes, the swill of the cloth
flowing over her breasts and her jeans gliding a little

at the waist, a slow texture rocking when she strode.
People look then ask, "What is it about her?" as they
did of Olenska in the brougham, behind the rain-stained
isinglass, the deep purple of her crushable velvet hat.

*T*hree

PARROTS

One day last June, blossoming near and far,
lust hugely itself. Morning of shimmering mirages.
Mirages flooding and trembling all points of view.
Heat and liquid lights. Heat and clear water
spilling over stones. Low tympanic rustlings,
percussive hushes and whispers. The green dew
of the diamond-studded grass. She came close
and my heart in its small coop pushed and rushed
frantic as forty parrots over a spill of crumbs.
Feathers of green and gold and scarlet. Wings
flapping, feathers falling, some drifting up
then vanishing behind white clouds. Cascades
of light when eyelids closed. Light that felt
silver and tasted of snow. The spirit opens
the mind on such a day, after it opens the heart.
Aphrodite plotted every move and approved the
performance. She wore her long tasseled shawl,
her beaded vest, her favorite leather sandals.
Lavender mist between low hills. Much later,
in the evening, after an afternoon of silky slow
touch kiss taste flesh and bone song, she slipped
away in that mist, pleased with her power,
laughing while crossing six rivers, twenty hills.

THE WOODEN EGG

I keep it on my writing desk to honor you,
and somewhere you are writing about it,
or rather, about the desire that ascended in you
the day you sought it.

In that town, nowhere decent to buy a gift,
not if you walked across the tarmac
of the parking lot into the glare-searing
mall, not if you drove to that dust-thick
card shop on the square.

Yet your fingers stretched for this made-in-the-
Philippines egg, hand-painted fans of palmettos
and banyan leaves splayed across a deep maroon.
I think you liked the heft and curl of it
cupped in your hand.

We stood on the threshold between two
rooms, May's brash noon light purling
through windows green with trumpet vine,
and beyond the screens, the rhythm of
white clapboard lines.

You proffered it shyly, I remember, and I did
not gaze at you deeply enough to speak
my full thanks, still, for the first time, I felt
your love made tangible in such a silence
 as sweeps through snow.

NOVEMBER

Now you are my November muse,
none so lovely—stark edges, pure relief,
sky clabbered then mottled then
tumultuous and streaked. You hum
the attenuated pleasures of the fading beech,
the bleaching pleasures of bulrush and reed.
Departing geese drag their victories
behind them. Shadows don dark capes,
shroud the wood. Pokeberries and sumac
bleed the thicket. Sibilant trickster of deep
connections, each hour you brush me
with your magic, unbud the would-be bloom
of true resolve, as bittersweet sweetens
the gloom. No orange-blossom or rose
or peony famed like the true-earth fragrance
come sharp between us when we fall.

THE BED OF MUSIC

We lie touching on the bed of music, lost
together, although you are in the Midwest
and I am in the Northeast, and two phalanxes

of weather stage maneuvers between us.
You breathe and I feel your breath moving
in me, my lungs fill when yours empty,

and so the violin concerto enters our speech
then enlarges our hearts to make room for
everyone Harmony wants us to remember

and forgive—and now one by one they come
and stand before us: only your line is not
as long as mine, and since you are more

self-sacrificing, you take my longer line
and forgive first my father for his blundering
ignorance, then my mother for her prudery and

concern with seemly appearances. You touch
his weary face and her ashen face after sensing
the grief and anguish that has kept house in

their bodies. You turn pale and tremble
from shouldering their pain. I turn to your
father who is still asleep having just entered

the world that bends and extends time—he is
forgiven for his routine absences and all he
never knew about your mother's tribulations—

his hand is still bloodied from a cardinal's
beak, he nods and smiles in his deep slumber.
Then our former spouses seek forgiveness,

and others we suffered to love us—one or two
who sated themselves without thinking. We
absolve them for staking the gamblers and

rogues of dispassion, the shysters of gossip.
It takes us all day and half the night. We are
spent as the hunter's cartridges—the music has

blessed us beyond our strength to forgive.
We are blank—and thin as the haze of stars.

THREE FULL SEASONS AND
ONE CUT SHORT

I lay down and lust lay its heavy embroidered
rug on me, imprinted its designs. An exalted silence.
No motion. So I said yes, windows open all night,
a mock-orange pleating its balm through your room.
Small creatures, fluster and flurry in tall grasses.
High summer and we tasted its fruit, tasted
each other until the corn cribs strained their wires
and the fields grew sheaves. Among gatherings
and flockings, we folded into one another. Sleep
and hunger contained us. Bittersweet cascaded
orange and red berries down the sides of trees;
the wavering *V*s of geese shirred the sky. Then
the great decapitator, frost. A commodious
polishing of air and a hush that measures snow,
measured us. We expected skaters to scratch
the pond. You scratched my thighs. But desire
dissolved when the freshets ran to fields and
the fields turned to mirrors. A clarifying blue.
An iris rinse. Solitude became finer and unbridled.
I wanted the compass and reach of that quiet,
or maybe I stopped liking something in you. I had
walked your ground almost a year, yielding one thing
then another. Call it a vanishing. I don't want forgiveness.
Who can prophesy delight or grief, the interior seasons?

They would go around noon, separated by a minute
or two, both of them working at the Academy then.
He wore sports jackets. She wore dresses and high
heels. They crossed Pennsylvania at 21st, entered
a lobby, rode up six flights. They were above
the Circle Theatre, all that spring showing
De Sica's *The Garden of the Finzi-Continis.*
Their friend Joseph rented this room for meditation:
A mattress, his blue satsang cushion mid-floor,
an incense boat, a small brass gong, a postcard
photo of his maharishi. The parquet was old,
scrubbed colorless. Through the slats at the
window—the White House, and beyond,
the Washington Monument, the Capitol dome.
The city abuzz with the word *impeachment,*
Nixon was that madman who schemed
five blocks east of them. In that room he
first entered her from behind. She was staring
across the floor at the blue cushion, the ridge
of his teeth scuffing the rim of her left ear,
his words lost, though of love. While they
were wholly transfixed by sensation in that lost
extravagant way, a bright wheat-colored light
unfolded across the walls and floor. The presence
Joseph had called so often to that place, must approve
of their passion— this new light, a sign of blessing.

This was the meaning settled on as they dressed.
At their peak, cherry and crabapple wavered above
beds of tulips, cast a delicate brume over the city.

A DELICATE HARMONIC

Was it October they walked the spit?
The evening warm and a breeze blowing enclosure.
They stayed until the moon rose, and walking back,
spoke only promises. He smoothed his perceptions
and folded them away like linens. Could he be more
amorphous, more diffuse, and still be said to be?
Through her he touches all women. She is conduit to
what is impossible, and when she lifts her shirt, he sees
his fingers tear roses apart. The good-bye-honey voice
that pours itself out continuously, the voice of partings.
Not wending, not an ambling fog, but views so unfocused
they meld back into themselves. Eaten away, the feeble
voice of exhaustion, the fevered voice of rage, and the still
more fevered voice of rage withheld, cut and singed by
hesitation. She is always leaving him for someone else—
the one she wants him to become—and he is not that,
he is himself, and she is herself, with only herself to
blame for her restlessness. She could out-see him, but
not out-speak him—not with his *nevers* and *never-agains*,
those final stops. The fog blurs all distinctions, as if the air
wished itself whitewashed and got its wish. Still it comes
with a holy patience. She feels stripped of a place to go,
and yearns to be called in heavy dusk by the voice
that calls in long intricate dreams, but that voice
vanished into rivers. It is death she wants to defeat, not him,

or maybe the death-in-them. Yet no way to press up against the flanks of death, no means to out-wit death. She can only cram more into her voice, find chinks in her prodigal fidelity.

THE REUNION

They had eaten seven peaches together,
    sitting there, slicing them idly, talking.
Light pooling under heavy trees. Crickets
    chaffing in the bright grass. It was too
much, suddenly, the richness of life, as if they

had come upon a spring afternoon in New Orleans,
    someone drawing them off the street and
into a courtyard for thick coffee and thin pastries.
    The bougainvillea laced with jasmine,
and, woven through the latticework, that

purple vine that blooms in clusters. Desire
    began to burn their tongues again
with its acrid ordained taste. A sanctified
    exchange. Twelve years, she counted
them, since she heard his voice last, his voice

that would wet her as she stood in her kitchen
    holding the phone, smiling, the street
through the window running to blur.
    No, not like anyone else's, but she
cannot describe his voice, nor the way

he would grab for her body before he had
    come entirely through the door.
Her need for summer inside her need
    for him—a rush, then silence, a running
down stairs, but no motion, no matter.

THE VISITATION

This is the penumbra of dawn when we sleep
In distant beds and I dream my dream of waking
You. Here, the harvest is almost through,

The earth open, cut, turned to the air, chaff blowing
About or starting to rot, the last flocks channeling
Down the flyway. You might see my back turn

In the pregnant swell of the curtain's silhouette,
The breeze as persistent as our desire for one another.
I am the one who brings you peace, you have said so

Until it is true. Here, as there, leaves scatter and skim,
And through them, the susurrations of restless squirrels,
And, more softly, field mice moving closer. Stay ten

Minutes under our white comforter, do not vitiate
Your pleasure waiting for me; I will come to you,
A succubus carrying honeyed tea, muffins,

Berries, and as you eat, I will lick your skin.
Remember how I would curl to you, my hand
Pressed to your head, as though I could pour out

More of myself than touch or taste or words can give?

ECONOMIES

In the country of my mother's life,
one always took the least expensive
choice—so when it came to death,

she chose cremation—no casket, plot,
or headstone. For all her economies
of touch and loss, pain and chance,

it seemed to me she paid the most.
She made decisions for the distance
they would last, and, to take up less

than a nutshell's space, she became dust
and had us feed her ashes to the sea.
But you have taught me more and most,

an economy of shore and sea and sky—
how standing there, one cannot think of less,
and the way, so often in your eyes,

a flood of tenderness threatens inundation.
You would have us spend ourselves as if we
had no shortages of lives. In this sufficiency,

multiplying harbors does not reduce
the sea, and here, on this strange
unstinting shore, only less is too expensive.

THE BANQUET

That day, with the lilacs finishing their bloom
and the leaves of newly full trees still bright green,
our table was on the lawn at noon, covered with
white linen, places set, two round vases of blue glass
flouncing the heavy blooms of peonies, the peonies
white and streaked with red. The music of a tenor
saxophone poured out the windows of our house,
our guests not yet come. We were waiting.
You said let's make love now, quickly, while there's
still time. Our bed by the window looked out over
the lawn and the table. High leaves spattered the
table with breeze-shimmering shadows. As we moved,
the silverware and glasses flashed the way the facets
of my ring flash when I roll my hand in sunlight,
so the table seemed to stand for our marriage,
the way my ring does, the long years of our happiness
funneled down from heaven and poured on this
table that stood in the flowering succor of summer light.
We were on the bed and on the table too, moving into
light and into shadow, the feast we had come to earth
to consume, being consumed, both of us host and guest
in easy exchange, our time here a taking and a giving back.

A SERIOUS SWEETNESS

When I say our life together has
a serious sweetness to it, I mean
the blackbirds in the trees this morning
babbling their leave-takings. I flapped
my arms and thousands rose to stream across
a cobbled sky. Yes, racy and ecstatic like that,
or soft and insistent the way at midnight
the cat paws the windowglass to be let in.
Someone I believed knew about relationships
once told me we'd taste this for a few years,
six at most, then marriage becomes
a semblance of itself, the sweetness vanishes,
and the soul, in aftermath, grows bitter—
unless it finds compensations. He thought
the snow that diamonds the frozen fields
is missed when freshets flow. But this
is windfall apples among frost-white grass,
the honey-sharp taste of the least bruised
I took from the orchard and polished
against your coat. Maybe it's all the pain
I've caused you through the years,
what you mean when you say, smiling,
it's never been dull living with you, that pain
somehow distilled, aged, clarified, to keep
this sweetness tart and nearly unbearable.

THE LAST OF OUR EMBRACES
TRANSFORMED FROM THE FIRST

I see our skulls, our grave bones move
when we step toward one another to kiss,
the dry hard whiteness coming close even
as our lips touch and our jawbones drop
for our mouths, our tongues. And I hear
that low hiss from the other side where
no one we know knows the amazement
of our love, or how costly it's been to keep
and grow. I don't care that death stands inside
of life, or that your head and chin, without flesh,
are as real to me as your tongue, or that moist
rim of tenderness I see in your eyes. I call this
the great night that steps into and out of us
constantly, trying us on like garments, counting
the hours until we become its complete possession.
The mystery is not that we die, we know this, we
take it like fall coming on, or winter—the mystery
is that love opens us again and again, brings us
back to tenderness and holiness, back to marrow.

THE SPINNING

The man and the woman celebrate their union
    as both a sound and smell, the sexual berry
in the mind, a chord held against high clear
    windows until light quakes—pleasure a palette,

a dollop of fresh paint. He wants her hands
    on his chest and back, belly and thighs—
tranquillity come to touch the sea, a clair-
    voyant soothsayer waiving guarantees.

She tweaks his nipples and they sting bell-clear.
    He tastes her sex until the feast the gods
have readied under his tongue is hot.
    If will is a saint's undoing, then this is what

they want: the last time like the first time,
    like the times in between, times at the window
over the backyards of noon, with three children
    in the basement playing gin rummy, and the

neighbor's lawn mower mowing—the goose
    and the gander flying through a plum sky—
evening and last light buffing the bark of the
    knobbiest beech—or the time by the stream

in the muddy-rivered south, cicadas slipping
   carapaces to the ground and his cries,
her cries, swollen inside the magnolia's damp
   blouses. He said he would inseminate

the words she shapes in her mouth—she said
   she would carry his words in her womb
and not shirk the largest subjects—infinity
   would split her bones before she would quit—

his eyes, the lamps that brighten each descent.
   A white garden inside the man, and a blue
garden, a scarlet garden, and a garden of stone.
   Violas and harpsichords inside her,

and festivals planned through six seasons.
   He walked long deer paths to find her,
she plumbed the want ads until a rasp said
   find him beside a statue of Bonaparte in

an Alsatian wood. As if something slipped from
   her heart and spilled itself on russet stones,
as if his semen coated the screen on which she
   projects herself—his foot went down where

a hoof went, where claw and talon long ago scarred
earth. His mouth is like that. Her mouth
on his, an enormity opening up, and the last planet
in the solar system begins its nebular spin.

NOTES

Ockham's Razor as mentioned in "The Past" refers to the name given to a corollary to one of the nominalistic doctrines promulgated by the English Scholastic philosopher, William of Ockham, which states that "entities must not be unnecessarily multiplied."

About "The Election": The death referred to is that of the poet, Anne Sexton, who died on October 4, 1974. The line, "Having for my soul's sake come to poetry," is from Robert Sargent, misquoted here as "sake," not "rescue" as is the original—the first line of his poem "The Lost Poems" published in his collection, *Aspects of a Southern Story* (Washington, D.C.: The Word Works, 1983).

The Juniper Prize
This volume is the twenty-third recipient
of the Juniper Prize presented annually by
the University of Massachusetts Press for
a volume of original poetry. The prize
is named in honor of Robert Francis
(1901–87), who lived for many years at
Fort Juniper, Amherst, Massachusetts.